For Richard – G.L

For Madeleine – J.M

MORE PRECIOUS THAN GOLD
by Gillian Lobel and Julie Monks
British Library Cataloguing in Publication Data
A catalogue record of this book is available from
the British Library.
ISBN 0 340 85486 3 (HB)
ISBN 0 340 85487 1 (PB)

First edition published 2003
10 9 8 7 6 5 4 3 2 1

Published by Hodder Children's Books
a division of Hodder Headline Limited
338 Euston Road London NW1 3BH

Printed in Hong Kong

More Precious Than Gold

Written by Gillian Lobel

Illustrated by Julie Monks

Hodder
Children's
Books

A division of Hodder Headline Limited

'Look! There it is!' Caspar pointed to the East.
'Nearer now, and brighter!'
Overhead the night sky blazed with a million stars.
But Caspar's star was different.
Low in the eastern sky it hung; huge, brilliant,
a burning white fire.

'Still a long way to go, my son.' Old Melchior
rested his arm on Caspar's shoulders.
'And so let us waste no more time!'
Balthazar stood tall in the stirrups,
starlight shimmering on his jewelled crown.

And so they rode on:
Melchior the wise, Balthazar the good,
and Caspar the youngest, kind and gentle.

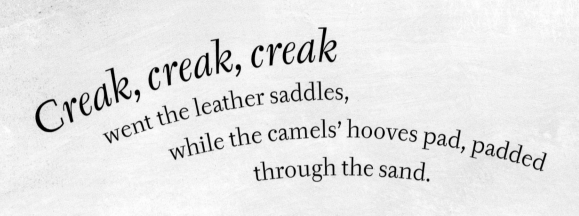

Creak, creak, creak
went the leather saddles,
while the camels' hooves pad, padded
through the sand.

And in the starlight three crowns glittered,
while the silver bells on the harness chimed softly.
Soon it would be time to rest,
before the sun set the desert on fire.

When dawn came, they were safe in the shade of palm trees. Melchior was soon asleep, his old bones aching with weariness. But Caspar sat a little while by the water, dreaming of his star – the star they had followed so long, the most exciting star the world had ever seen, that promised something wonderful, the child born to be King of Kings. He rested his head on a stone, lost in the wonder of it. Suddenly something moved!

A lizard flicked out a long tongue,
and tried to move away.
Bright scales burned gold in the sunlight.
Then Caspar saw the deep gash on its leg.

'Why, little one, that is a sore cut!'
Gentle hands reached out, and the lizard
suffered itself to be touched.
'This needs some of your ointment, brother!'
Caspar carried the wounded lizard to Balthazar.
'My ointment – the precious myrrh –
for a lizard!'
'Come brother, just a little. You have plenty
for the child.'

Suddenly Balthazar laughed.
'Oh Caspar, what shall we do
with you! Myrrh for a lizard!'
But he went to his
saddlebag, and
drew out the
precious casket.
As he unfastened
the gold clasps,
a strange scent
filled the air.

Caspar took the tiniest smear on his finger. Gently he stroked it onto the lizard's wound.

The little creature quivered slightly, but lay still. Then Caspar lapped it in leaves, and laid it in the cool of his saddlebag.

And in the heat of the day, they all slept: Melchior the wise,
Balthazar the good, Caspar the kind, and the little sand lizard,
until sunset streaked the sand with red and gold.
Then the three kings saddled their camels,
drank deeply from the pool, and set out.

Low in the eastern sky the star arose, closer now,
pulsing with a strange blue light.

All wrapped in starry silence they rode,
and the only sound was the creak of the saddlebags,
and the pad, pad of the camels' hooves.

And as the sky turned silver they saw rough grasses
under their feet, and found they were climbing out
of the desert into the hills.
'I will search for a stream.' Caspar leaped lightly over the
rocks. 'Be sure to save me some dates for my breakfast!'

Soon he was at the top of the hill. Down there in the valley – surely that was a little town! White roofs shone in the sunlight. He scrambled back down to the others.

Then he saw her, at the foot of an olive tree: a dove who did not fly away. Caspar bent down and touched the soft white feathers. She was warm! Gently he lifted her and tucked her into his robe.

'Have you found water, brother?' Balthazar was anxious. 'No, but I have seen a little town, not far away where we can find food and drink – and I found this too!' Caspar held out the dove in his cupped hands.

He poured a thin trickle of water into a silver cup, and stroked his wet fingers against the bird's neck. Her wings quivered for a second.

'We need every drop of our water, my son,' said Melchior gravely, but there was a faint smile about his lips.
'See, her wing is damaged.' Caspar's gentle fingers opened the fan of feathers. 'I will make a splint.'

And he rummaged in his saddlebag.

'Oh Caspar, whatever shall we do with you!' sighed
Balthazar. So the dove joined the sand lizard on the soft
blanket inside the saddlebags, and they set off towards the
little town: Melchior the wise, Balthazar the good, Caspar
the kind, the little sand lizard, and the soft white dove.

Down in the valley the town baked in the heat of the day. In a back street a little cat crept into an open door. She was tired and hungry – oh so hungry! She had not eaten for two days, and her bones stuck out from her faded silver coat. Something smelled delicious! She leaped onto a table. At last, a plate of fresh fish!

She began to tear at the food.

'Get out, filthy cat!' A stone caught her sharply. She ran, her fur fluffed with terror, until she could go no further. She collapsed, panting, under a rock. She stretched to lick her back, where the warm blood was flowing.

For a long time she lay, till the shaking stopped.
Then she crawled out in search of water. Painfully,
she limped downhill, towards the stream. Then
she stiffened, her nostrils quivering. What a strange
smell! She slunk through the grasses, afraid to
go forward. But she was so thirsty!

'Why, little one, you are injured!'
She shrank back, her back arched,
ready to spit and claw, waiting for
the stones to fly.

'Come on, sweetheart, I won't hurt you.'
She froze, uncertain. Long ago there had
been a kind voice, and warm goat's milk to
drink. Her mouth watered at the memory.
'Come on, little mother!' The soft voice stroked
her sore body.

A hand touched her –
oh so gently – and she did
not run away. Then a piece of
dried fish appeared on the ground.
Ravenously she tore at it. And all the time the
kind hand soothed her fur, and warmed her through.

'Whatever is it now, my son?'
Old Melchior sighed.
'A cat, father, sore wounded –
and I think she carries little ones!
I will need some ointment, Balthazar!'
And so the little cat was soothed and
her wounds cleaned and dressed
with precious ointment.
'I will take her with me until
she is stronger,' said Caspar.
'Oh Caspar, whatever shall we do with you!'
sighed Melchior and Balthazar.

And so they rested from the heat of the day, until their star arose in the east again, huge, brilliant, nearer: Melchior the wise, Balthazar the good, Caspar the kind, the little sand lizard, the soft white dove, and the silver cat.

And now the star seemed to move before them, drawing them on.

In one of Caspar's saddlebags, the dove and the lizard slept and grew strong, while in the other, the little silver cat lay curled, breathing in the sweet perfume of incense. And in the comforting night, her three kittens were born; one gold as the sand, one black as the midnight sky, and one silver as the star above them.

N ow the star was right overhead. Caspar
thought his heart would break for joy.
In front of them was a poor stable, built into
the hillside. And they knew this was the right place.

Then the camels sank to their knees, and
the three kings went towards the doorway.

And there they found the Child, lying in the manger, with his mother Mary, while Joseph watched over them.

And they knelt before him, and gave him gifts;
gold from Melchior, fit for a king, myrrh from Balthazar,
for the healing of sorrows, and frankincense from Caspar,
the sweet perfume of kindness.

And as Caspar knelt in worship, the dove flew
out of the saddlebag, and hovered over their heads.
Suddenly, the stable seemed full of shimmering wings.
A gold sand lizard crept gratefully into the warmth
and light, and a little silver cat and her three
kittens blinked in the brightness.
'Oh *Caspar*!' said Balthazar and Melchior.
And Caspar hung his head for shame.

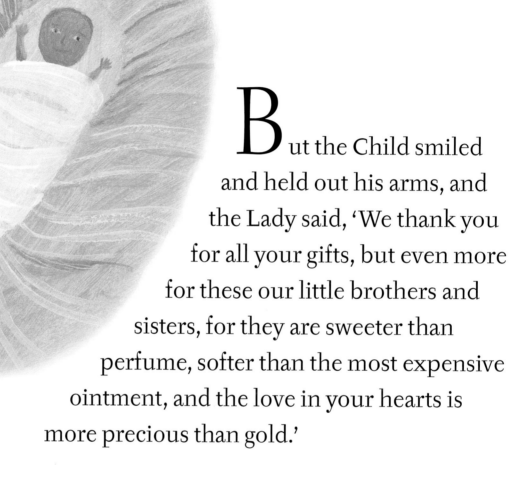

But the Child smiled
and held out his arms, and
the Lady said, 'We thank you
for all your gifts, but even more
for these our little brothers and
sisters, for they are sweeter than
perfume, softer than the most expensive
ointment, and the love in your hearts is
more precious than gold.'